A special thanks to the wonderful
people of the Pacific Islands for
inspiring us on this journey as we bring
the world of *Moana* to life.

randomhousekids.com

ISBN 978-0-7364-3602-1

Printed in the United States of America

10 9 8 7 6 5 4 3 2 1

DISNEY
MOANA

Adapted by
Bill Scollon

Illustrated by
the Disney Storybook Art Team

A GOLDEN BOOK • NEW YORK

In the beginning, there was nothing but ocean. Then the mother island, Te Fiti, emerged. From her heart, all life was created.

One of the new islands was called **Motunui**. Protected from the ocean waves by a barrier reef, the island was a paradise for its people.

And all those who called Motunui home were bound together by traditions and legends.

One of the most famous legends told of Maui, a shape-shifting demigod with a magical fishhook. Like many others, he believed Te Fiti's heart held life-giving power. Taking the form of a hawk, Maui flew to the mother island and

stole the heart of Te Fiti!

The children of the village sat spellbound as Gramma Tala continued her story. "Maui tried to escape," she said. "But he was confronted by Te Kā, a demon of earth and fire!"

In the battle, Maui lost both the **heart** and his **fishhook**. With the heart gone, a terrible darkness spread across the world.

"It will continue to spread," Gramma Tala said, "draining the life from island after island!"

The other children were scared, but Moana loved the stories!

As the other children wailed, little Moana wandered to the ocean shore. She saw a baby turtle in trouble, so she helped it to the water. As the turtle swam away, Moana saw a pretty shell. She picked it up, and the ocean backed away to reveal more shells.

Moana giggled as the ocean presented her with a **beautiful green stone!**

When Chief Tui called for his daughter, the ocean gently set Moana back on the beach before he arrived. And as Tui lifted Moana, the little girl accidentally dropped the ocean's gift.

Gramma Tala saw everything and smiled. She knew what the stone was, and she took it. When the time was right, she'd return it to Moana.

As Moana grew, so did her love for **Motunui and its people,** as well as her connection to the ocean. Chief Tui made sure his daughter understood and appreciated all the wonderful things about the village. Inside their protected bay, the people were safe and had everything they needed. Tui told Moana she would find happiness right where she was. She would make a wonderful **chief** when she was older.

When Moana turned sixteen, Chief Tui took her to the
island's highest peak. That was where every chief who had
come before had placed a stone.

"Like I did, like my dad did, and his dad before him," Tui
told Moana. "When you are ready, you will add your stone to
this mountain and raise our island higher. It's time to be who
the people need you to be."

Moana still felt drawn to the ocean. She heard at the village council that fish were growing scarce in the bay, and she wondered if there were more fish in the open sea.

Even though the villagers were forbidden to sail across the reef because it was too dangerous, Moana decided to try. But waves wrecked the boat and tossed her back to shore!

Moana felt discouraged. Perhaps it was time to give up on the sea and place her rock on the mountain. But Gramma Tala encouraged Moana to listen to her heart. Then she took Moana to a hidden cavern.

"What's in there?" asked Moana.

Gramma Tala smiled. "The answer to the question 'Who are you meant to be?'"

Inside the cavern were dozens of huge, ancient, sea-voyaging boats!

"We were voyagers!" cried Moana. "Why did we stop?"

"Maui is to blame," explained Gramma Tala. After he stole the heart, darkness fell and monsters prowled the ocean. To protect the people, ancient chiefs forbade voyaging.

"The darkness has continued to spread," said Gramma, pointing to blackened trees around them. "Chasing our fish and draining the life from island after island." She looked at Moana. "But one day, someone will deliver Maui across the ocean to restore the heart."

Then she gave Moana the stone she'd been keeping safe: the heart of Te Fiti! **"The ocean chose you."**

Soon afterward, Gramma Tala became very ill. She pressed her necklace into Moana's hand—it would hold the heart of Te Fiti while Moana traveled.

Quickly, Moana chose a canoe from the cavern and set off. Far out at sea, she discovered a stowaway—a rooster named Heihei.

Moana barely knew how to sail. Then a storm hit!

The storm tossed Moana's boat onto a rocky island—**Maui's island!** He'd been marooned for a thousand years, looking for a way to escape so he could recover his magical fishhook. Without the hook, he had no shape-shifting powers.

Moana told Maui he must go with her to restore the heart of Te Fiti. But Maui was only interested in bragging about his great feats—like pulling up the sky, lassoing the sun, and bringing fire to humans.

"You're welcome!" he said.

Maui took Moana's boat and left her behind. "Enjoy the island!"
he shouted. Moana swam after Maui, but he was too far ahead.
Suddenly, the ocean lifted Moana up and set her on the boat.
Maui was speechless!

Moana held up the heart. **"I am Moana of Motunui,"** she said bravely. **"You will journey to Te Fiti and restore the heart!"**

Maui backed away. "That's not a heart, it's a curse!"

Without warning, a spear slammed into the canoe! It was the **Kakamora,** vicious little bandits wearing coconut armor. They wanted the heart.

The bandits swarmed the boat. In the commotion, the heart fell out of Moana's necklace—and Heihei gobbled it up!

A bandit snatched the dim-witted rooster and ran back to his ship. Moana chased him, batted the Kakamora out of the way, and grabbed Heihei. She returned to her canoe just as the rooster coughed up the heart.

But the Kakamora boats were still after them.

Grabbing the oar and the lines to the sail, **Maui expertly sailed out of danger!**

After defeating the Kakamora, Moana couldn't wait to battle Te Kā and restore the heart. But Maui just wanted his fishhook back.

Moana had an idea. "We get your hook, then save the world. Deal?"

Maui hesitated, but Moana pointed out that he'd be a hero if he restored the heart. "Deal," he said at last.

Moana asked Maui to teach her how to sail. "You'll never be a wayfinder," he scoffed.

The ocean didn't like the sound of that. It picked up one of the Kakamora blow darts and jabbed Maui!

Maui collapsed, temporarily paralyzed except for his head. **"Really?"** he asked the ocean.

"If you can talk, you can teach," said Moana with a laugh.

Maui finally agreed, but only because he had to!

Maui knew that Tamatoa, a monstrous crab who loved collecting shiny things, had his hook. But Tamatoa's lair was under the ocean in **Lalotai,** the dreaded realm of monsters!

There was only one way into the mysterious world: scale a thousand-foot cliff and jump down a chute all the way through the ocean!

Lalotai was a dark and mysterious land, full of glowing plants and geysers that blasted through the watery ceiling.

It wasn't long before Maui spotted his fishhook stuck to Tamatoa's shell, along with the rest of the giant crab's collection of shiny items. Maui charged in and grabbed his hook.

"It's Maui time!" he cried. Then Maui tried to shape-shift into a hawk. Instead, he became a bug, then a pig!

"This never happens to me!" the demigod said in shock.

Tamatoa pinned Maui to the ground. To distract the monster, Moana held up the heart of Te Fiti, then dropped it into a crevice. Tamatoa skittered after the shiny stone while Moana ran to her injured friend.

But Moana had tricked Tamatoa—she still had the heart! She helped Maui escape before the angry crab could grab them.

Moana guided Maui onto a geyser hole. **Whoosh!** The geyser blasted them to the surface!

Moana knew Maui needed to regain his full strength to fight Te Kā, but the demigod couldn't master the hook's shape-shifting power. It seemed like Maui was giving up.

As he moped, Moana asked about one of his special tattoos.

"I had human parents," explained Maui. "They didn't want me. They threw me into the sea. Like I was nothing."

"You're not nothing," said Moana. "Maybe the whole reason the ocean sent me here is to help you see that."

Moana's words touched Maui. He began practicing with the hook and got better and better. And as Maui regained his shape-shifting abilities, he taught Moana more about wayfinding.

At last, Maui felt ready. Moana used her new wayfinding
skills to sail her boat straight to Te Fiti. Clouds of smoke
and ash rose over the barrier islands, hiding Te Kā.

Moana gave Maui the heart and smiled. "Go save the
world," she said.

Maui turned into a hawk and flew off to restore the heart of Te Fiti. But suddenly, **Te Kā—the lava monster—** burst through the clouds and knocked Maui out of the sky!

"No!" screamed Moana. Quickly, she sailed in and pulled Maui from the water.

Moana steered toward a narrow gap between the barrier islands. She was heading back into battle!

"We won't make it," said Maui. "Turn around!"

Just then, Te Kā brought down a fist to destroy the boat. Maui blocked it with his hook!

The shock wave blasted Moana and Maui far out into the ocean. The boat was in shambles, and Maui's fishhook was cracked.

"We can fix it," Moana told him.

"It was made by the gods. You can't fix it!" Maui refused to go back. "Without my hook, I'm nothing!" he said. He was afraid another fight with Te Kā would shatter his hook completely.

Moana pleaded with him to stay. **"The ocean chose me,"** she said.

"It chose wrong," Maui replied angrily. Then he shape-shifted into a hawk and flew away.

Moana yelled at the ocean. "Why did you bring me here?" she asked, sobbing. "Choose someone else!" Then she dropped the heart of Te Fiti back into the ocean.

Just then, a glowing manta ray swam by. A moment later, the spirit of Gramma Tala appeared on the boat! "I never should have put so much on your shoulders," she said, wiping away Moana's tears. "If you want to go home, I will be with you."

But Moana could not make herself turn the boat around. **"Listen to the voice inside,"** Gramma said. **"Do you know who you are?"**

Moana began slowly. "I am the daughter of the village chief," she said. "We are descended from voyagers." Moana's voice grew stronger as the spirits of her voyaging ancestors appeared near the boat. "I have fought with monsters. I am all these things and more. **I am Moana!**"

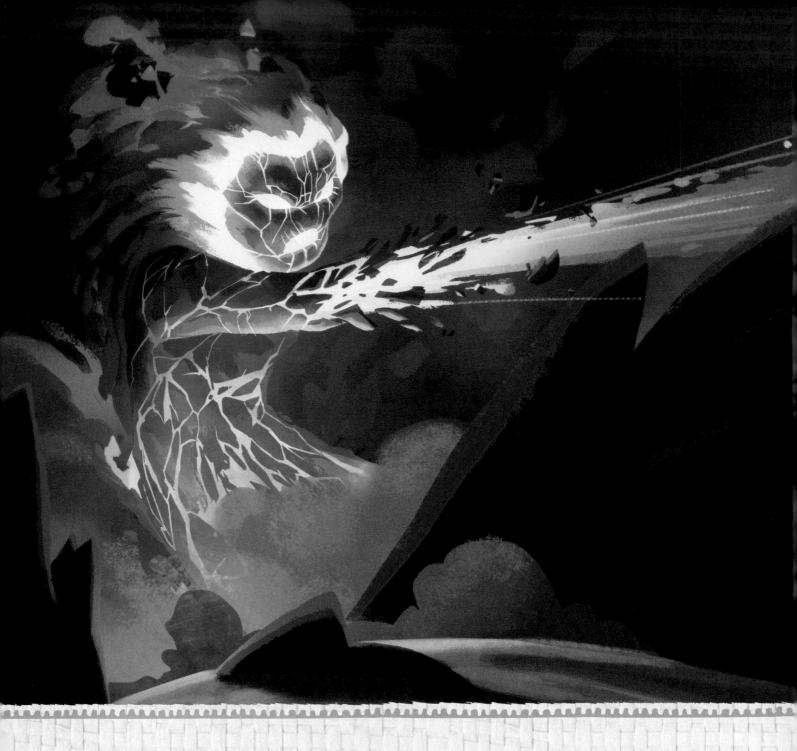

Moana dove into the ocean, swimming deeper and deeper in search of the heart. At last she saw it, glowing at the bottom of the sea. Moana kept going until finally she had the heart! When she came back up, Gramma Tala was gone.

Moana knew what she had to do. She repaired the boat and sailed back to face Te Kā on her own. She steered toward an opening between the barrier islands, heading for Te Fiti.

Moana noticed that Te Kā couldn't move through the water. That meant that if she got past the barrier islands, she'd make it to Te Fiti.

But the lava monster brought down a fist again. Moana dodged the blow and turned toward another gap. When Te Kā cut her off, Moana doubled back. **It was all part of her plan!**

At last, Moana made it through, but Te Kā launched a lava ball that capsized her boat.

Te Kā's hand was poised over Moana, ready to deliver a final blow. Suddenly, Maui appeared and knocked the monster's fist away!

"Maui!" cried Moana. "But your hook . . ."

Maui held up the cracked hook and nodded. "Some things are more important," he said. "I've got your back. **Go save the world!**"

"Thank you," said Moana.

Maui smiled.

"You're welcome!"

Moana reached Te Fiti and scrambled up a slope. But something was wrong. The island was gone! There was no place to put the heart!

She turned and saw that Te Kā had completely smashed Maui's fishhook. And for the first time, Moana noticed a glowing spiral on Te Kā's chest.

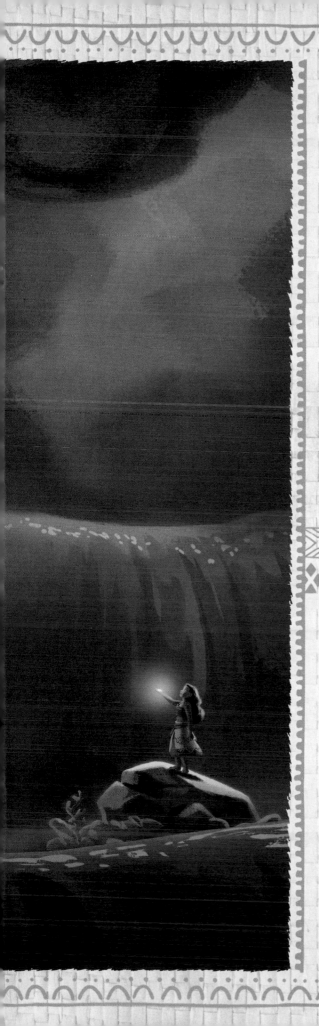

Moana held the heart of Te Fiti over her head and spoke to the ocean. "Let her come to me."

The water parted, opening a path that led straight to Te Kā. The monster raced toward Moana!

Very calmly, Moana began to sing. Her song echoed what Gramma Tala had taught her and what she'd learned about herself.

The words seemed to affect Te Kā, who slowed down.

"I know who you are," Moana whispered. Then she placed the heart in the glowing spiral . . . and **Te Fiti** emerged!

Maui apologized to Te Fiti. "What I did was . . .
I have no excuse," he said. "I did it for myself, and
I'm sorry. You may smite me now."

Te Fiti brought down her fist, but not in anger. In
her palm was Maui's fishhook, completely restored!
With love, Te Fiti then set Moana on the beach, where
her boat, covered in flowers, was ready to sail home.

Moana gave Maui a **hug**. "You could come with
me. My people are going to need a master wayfinder."

"They already have one," said Maui. A tattoo of
Moana the wayfinder appeared over his heart!

All across the ocean, life returned. The spreading darkness was gone. On Motunui, the land turned green and lush. Fish returned to the bay.

The whole village joined Moana's parents at the water's edge to welcome Moana and Heihei home.

At last, Moana was ready to become a leader and place her stone with those of the other chiefs. But for Moana, it wasn't a stone—it was a conch shell.

The islanders were inspired and remembered who they were: **voyagers!** Together, they repaired the ancient boats and headed into the open ocean for a new era of exploration, led by a master wayfinder.

She was Moana!